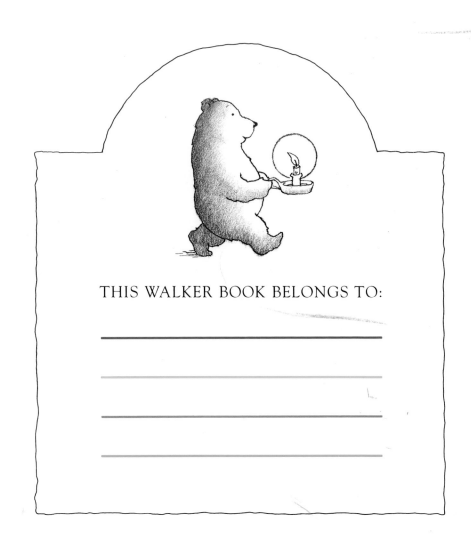

THIS WALKER BOOK BELONGS TO:

_____

_____

_____

_____

First published 2001 by Walker Books Ltd
87 Vauxhall Walk, London SE11 5HJ

This edition published 2002

2 4 6 8 10 9 7 5 3

Text © 2001 Claire Masurel
Illustrations © 2001 Kady MacDonald Denton

This book has been typeset in Godlike

Printed in Hong Kong

British Library Cataloguing in Publication Data:
a catalogue record for this book is
available from the British Library

ISBN 0-7445-8925-8

Two Homes

Claire Masurel *illustrated by* Kady MacDonald Denton

WALKER BOOKS
AND SUBSIDIARIES
LONDON • BOSTON • SYDNEY

Here I am! I am Alex.

This is Daddy.

And this is Mummy.

Daddy lives here.
Sometimes I'm with Daddy.

Mummy lives there.
Sometimes I'm with Mummy.

So … I have *two homes!*

I have *two* front doors.

My coat goes here.

My coat goes there.

I have *two* rooms.

My room at Daddy's.

My room at Mummy's.

I have *two* favourite chairs.

A rocking chair at Daddy's.

A soft chair at Mummy's.

I have lots of friends.

Friends come and play at Daddy's.

Friends come and play at Mummy's.

I have *two* kitchens.

Daddy and I cook here.

Mummy and I cook there.

I have *two* bathrooms.

I have a toothbrush at Daddy's.

I have a toothbrush at Mummy's.

And I have *two* telephone numbers.

Mummy rings me at Daddy's house.

Daddy rings me at Mummy's house.

I love Daddy.

And I love Mummy.
No matter where I am.

We love you, Alex.

We love you wherever we are.

And we love you wherever you are.